This Little Tiger book belongs to:

_____

_____

_____

To MJF

LITTLE TIGER PRESS
An imprint of Magi Publications
1 The Coda Centre, 189 Munster Road,
London SW6 6AW
www.littletigerpress.com

First published in Great Britain 2005
This edition published 2006

2 4 6 8 10 9 7 5 3

A CIP catalogue record for
this book is available from
the British Library
Printed in China
ISBN 978-1-84506-201-9

The Fantastic Mr Wani

Kanako Usui

> Mr Wani
>
> Hello Mr Wani! We are having a party at 11 o'clock on Sunday. Please come and join us!
>
> The Froggies

LITTLE TIGER PRESS
London

Mr Wani the crocodile was in a hurry.
He was almost late for a party in town.
So he started to run.

He ran and ran, faster and faster . . .

but his little legs couldn't keep up!

Bang!

He tripped,
tumbled
and bounced . . .

Meanwhile, a little way down the road,
four mice were also on their way to a party.

Smash!

Out of nowhere Mr Wani came crashing down on the unsuspecting mice!

"I'm sorry I squashed you," said Mr Wani.
"I'm rushing to a party. I'm worried that I will be late.
I just don't know what to do!"

The mice were very kind, and they put
their heads together for him.

"I've an idea!" cried Miss Mouse.
"Let's use these

balloons!

You can fly to the party!"

Town ⇨

The mice tied the balloons to Mr Wani's mouth.
"You are clever, Miss Mouse!" said Mr Wani.
"If I fly, I'll certainly get to the party on time!"
Mr Wani began to run . . . and . . .

took off!

Up in the sky, Mrs Crow was rushing to a party when she came across what she thought were lots of colourful floating sweets.

"Ooh! Delicious!"
she said, and she swooped down to gobble them up!

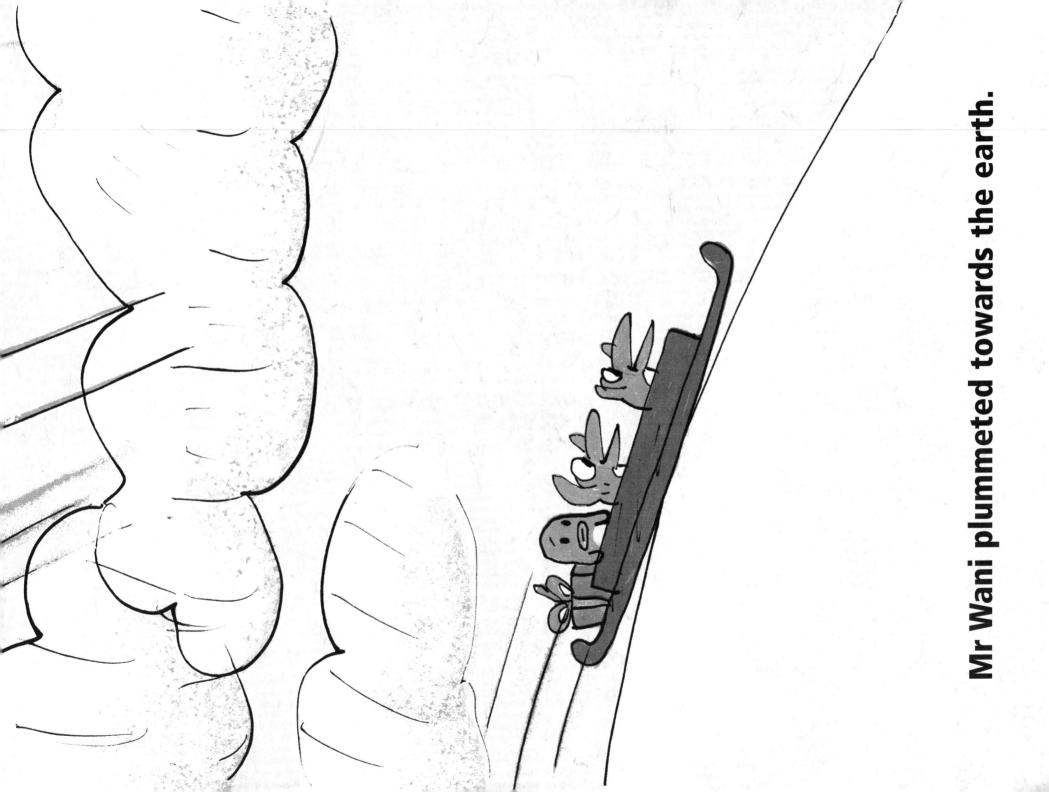

Mr Wani plummeted towards the earth.

Crash!

Mr Wani landed right on top of three penguins!

The penguins were very upset because Mr Wani had broken their sledge.

"Oh no! What can we do? How will we get to the party?" said the penguins sadly.

Mr Wani felt sorry for them. So he offered to take them down the hill.

But the Mr Wani sledge went

faster **and faster and faster!**
Finally it flew out of control and the penguins
were thrown off high into the sky!

Mr Wani sped on . . .

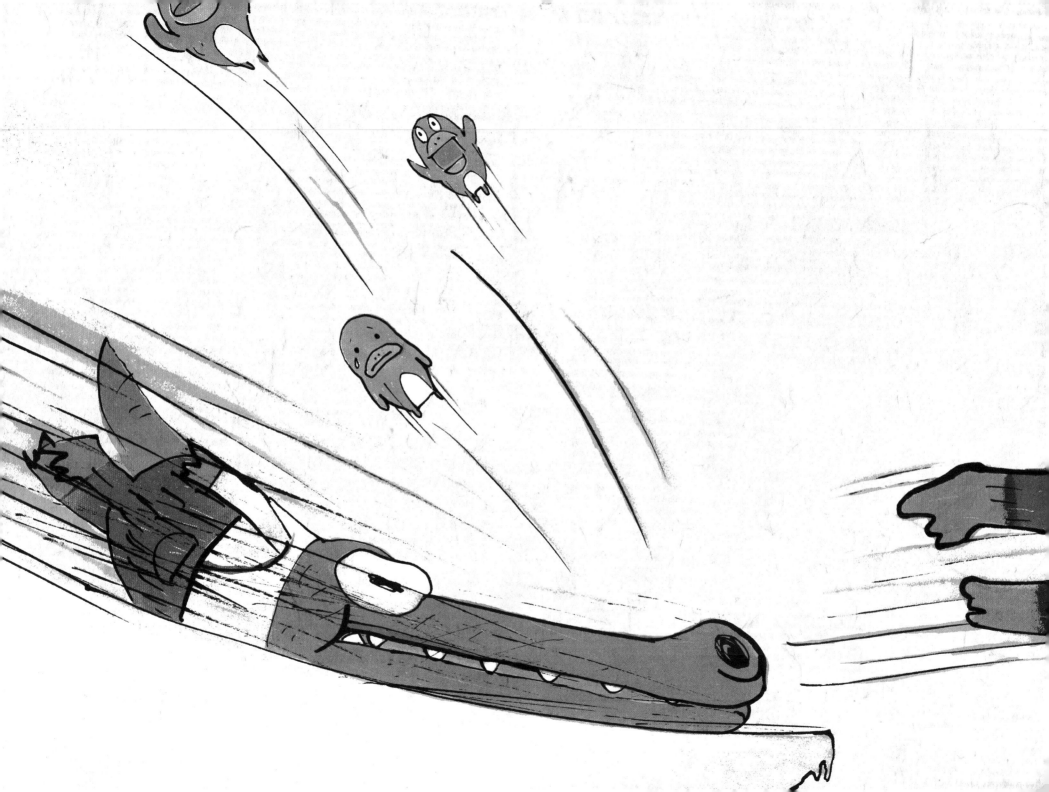

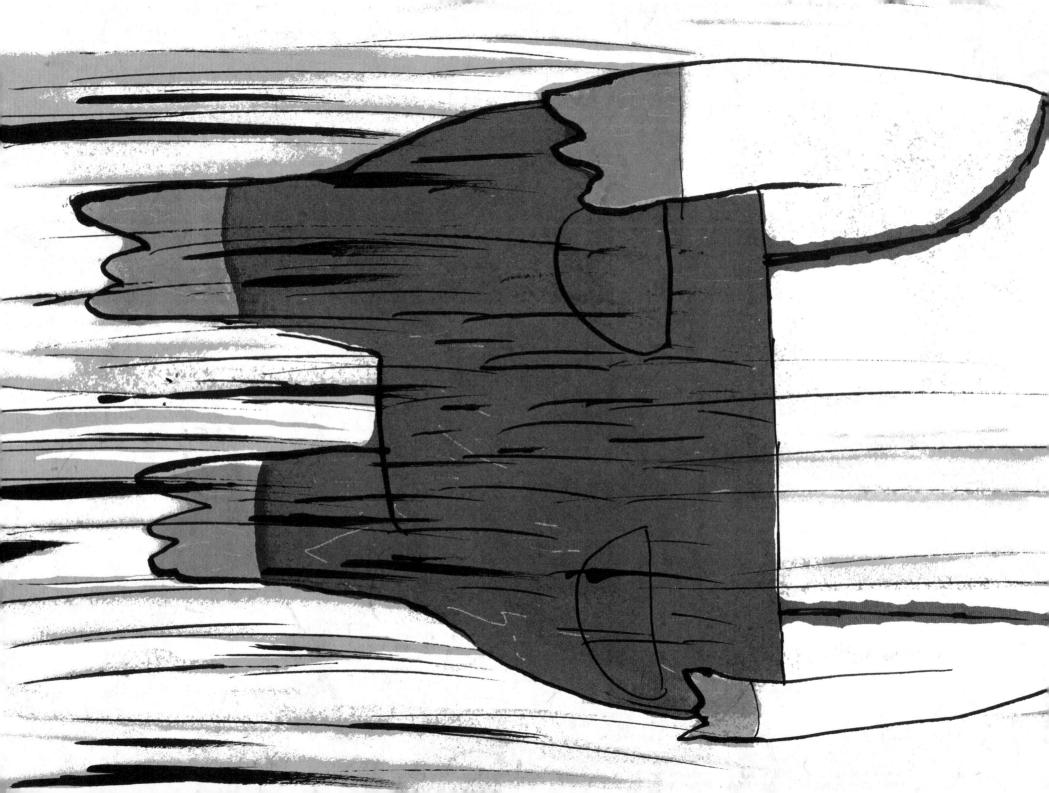

Bump! into Mr Elephant's rump.

Screech!

Mr Elephant skidded to a stop.

Mr Wani was flung into the air
and landed right on top of
a prickly hedgehog!

Mr Wani bounced and bounced, higher and higher.

"Yikes!" he cried . . .

Froggies

. . . and landed right in the middle of the party!

"Hi, Mr Wani! Have a crisp," said the Froggies.
Mr Wani's new friends were there too.
The party went on for the whole
day and they all had a

wonderful time.

In the evening, after everyone had left,
Mr Tortoise turned up.
He was very, very late . . .

More **fantastic** books to make you **giggle!**

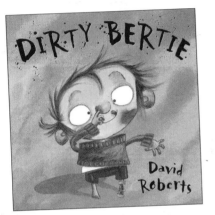

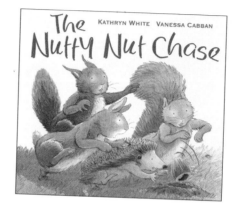

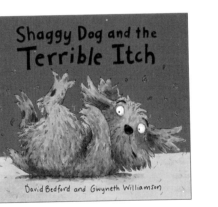
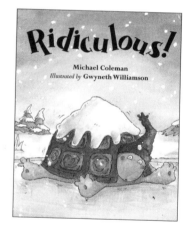